Leonie Lord

SOFA DOG

ALISON GREEN BOOKS

This is me . . .

. . . and this is my sofa.

And when I say "my sofa", I mean **my** sofa. There's no room for anyone else –

except for my human.

Her name's Sophie.
We love our sofa time.

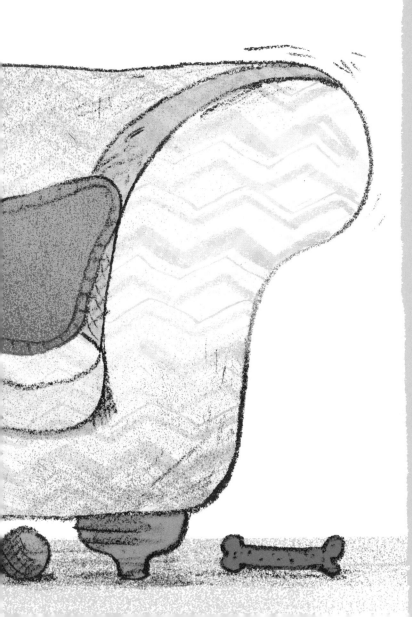

But then we hear:

click
clack
flap!

And Sophie says:

"Budge up, Sofa Dog!
Next door's cats have
come to play."

So now there's **me**,
and my **human**,
and two **cats** –
and there's no room for anyone else!

But then we hear:

Ding-dong!
Ding-dong!
Ding-dong!

And Sophie says:

"Budge up, Sofa Dog!
My three aunties have come to stay.
They're all knitting me jumpers . . .

. . . and one for you, too!"

So now there's **me**,
and my **human**,
and two **cats**,
and three **aunties** –
and there's no room
for anyone else!

But then we hear:

RAT-A-
TAT-TAT!

And
RAT-A-
TAT-TAT!

And
RAT-A-TAT-
TAT-TAT
-TAT!

And Sophie says:

"Budge up, Sofa Dog!

My friend Polly's come round
with her prize-winning **pony**.

"And I've been sent a box of **rabbits!**

"And Grandpa's arrived
from Bavaria, with his amazing
orangutan oompah band.

"And I've won a **panda**
in a competition!"

So now . . .

. . . there's **me**,
and my **human**,
and two **cats**,
and three **aunties**,
and seven **rabbits**,
and Polly with her **pony**,
and one **grandpa**,
and one amazing
**orangutan
oompah band**,
and the **panda**
(who wants a pillow fight.)

Oh, and one more
little guest that
nobody's noticed . . .
a teeny, tiny **flea**.

And there's **no room** for **anyone else** . . .

. . . not even me!

BUMP!

And Sophie says:

"Everyone who's scratching

has to go home at once!"

So off they all go.

Now there's lots more room on the sofa.

And I've found a lovely piece of **cheese** in the bin.

Ooooh!

Cheese on the sofa!
What a perfect
combination.

I eat my cheese in peace, and
catch up on a little sofa time.

But it can be lonely on the sofa, all by yourself.

Then I hear:

Stomp!
Stomp!
Stomp!

"Sofa Dog! Where ARE you?"

"There you are!" says Sophie.
"Budge up, Sofa Dog. I like it when
it's just you and me.

"And there's **no room for anyone else!**"

For Steve and Lavender

First published in the UK in 2017 by Alison Green Books
An imprint of Scholastic Children's Books
Euston House, 24 Eversholt Street, London NW1 1DB
A division of Scholastic Ltd

www.scholastic.co.uk

London – New York – Toronto – Sydney – Auckland
Mexico City – New Delhi – Hong Kong

Copyright © 2017 Leonie Lord

HB ISBN: 978 1 407171 83 8
PB ISBN: 978 1 407171 84 5